Legends from Vamland

Vladimir Colin

Legends from Vamland

Adapted and Retold by Luiza Carol

Illustrated by Octavian Ion Penda

CENTER FOR
Romanian
S T U D I E S

CENTER FOR ROMANIAN STUDIES

Las Vegas ◆ Oxford ◆ Palm Beach

Published in the United States of America by
Histria Books, a division of Histria LLC
7181 N. Hualapai Way, Ste. 130-86
Las Vegas, NV 89166, USA
www.histriabooks.com

The Center for Romanian Studies is an imprint of Histria Books. Titles published under the imprints of Histria Books are distributed worldwide through the Casemate Group.

Second Printing, 2020

Library of Congress Control Number: 2019954880

ISBN 978-973-9432-20-7 (hardcover)
ISBN 978-1-59211-051-3 (paperback)
ISBN 978-1-59211-052-0 (ebook)

About the Book
and its Author

This book is the most beautiful story I have read about the human being's fight against fear.

Its author. Vladimir Colin (1921-1991). was a Romanian Jew who lived in Bucharest. Like all European Jews of his generation, he could be called a survivor. He had a direct experience of some of the most terrible social and political upheavals in the history of mankind and it is from such a background that this wonderful story arose. Before the war. Vladimir Colin had graduated the German School and then he studied literature and philosophy at the University of Bucharest. His sound knowledge of world's philosophics and history of religions lay at the basis of his further interest in folklore traditions as contained in fairy-tales all over the world. Besides writing fairy-tales and children's stories. Vladimir Colin was also the author of a great many science-fiction novels, historical novels, fantastical novels and short-stories, many of which were translated into German. French. Italian, Russian, Polish. Czech. Slovak, and Vietnamese.

Legends from Vamland was first printed in 1961 when the author was 40. By then he had already pub-

lished and broadcast several dozens of wonderful fairy-
tales and he had already won Romania's prestigious
prize for literature. In writing this book, Colin
behaved like a magician who blended in his melting pot
popular legends and myths from all places and times:
old Romanian fairy-tales like "The Magical Bird" and
"Youth-Without-Old-Age and Life-Without-Death."
the Arab legend of the Ghost in the Brass Pot (from
The 1001 Nights), the Tartar legend about a country
called Van ("The Story of Happiness"), the Jewish legend about the Golem, the Chinese myth about Pan-ku
the cosmic man are only a few of them. One can find
here echoes of the best literary pieces ever written in
all cultures: Ovid's *Metamorphoses*. Shakespeare's *A
Midsummer Night's Dream*. Goethe's *Faust*. Wag-
ner's *The Ring of the Nibelungen*. "The Book of Job."
"The Gospel of St. John," and Macpherson's *Poems of
Ossian* to name but a few. In fact, the areas of the sym-
bols overlap to such a degree, that one can hardly find
any noble and beautiful human aspiration in all the cultures of the world whose reflection is not to be found
in *Legends from Vamland*. In a way. the book was in-
tended to be a work of science-fiction too: there is a
would-be "preface" in which the author talks about the
"scientific" researches made by scientists who have
translated the texts from the would-be Vamitic language. So. what we are given is the image of the spiri-
tual life of an imaginary people from an imaginary

land. The result of this extraordinary concoction is an amazing magical cocktail of splendid originality.

I venture to formulate the hypothesis that Vladimir Colin used some Hebrew words when he named his characters of Vamland. The following might be the proofs:

1. The author was born on May 1. 1921. The same date on the Hebrew calendar was Nissan 23. 5681. The name of the month "Nissan" has the same letters as SAIAN, the god of the sun in Vamland. Moreover, according to Kabbalistic numerology, the number 23 means "The Royal Star of the Lion."

2. VIHTA, the name of the fume bird of love, may be written in Hebrew with the same letters as the name IAHVE plus the letter T which is the Hebrew ending for feminine nouns. Did the author think of a feminine aspect of God?

3. MASTARA, the name of the goddess of death, has the same Hebrew grammatical root as "mastira" which means "(she) hides."

4. In the story. PIL. the god of tricks, was said to have got his name by inversion from his original name LIP. In Hebrew the word "lip" means "fiber" and the word "pil" means "elephant." Did the author mean to say that a small trick may sometimes be turned into something enormous?

5. ORMAG, the name of the evil god of Vamland, has the same Hebrew letters as the word "gamour" which means "finished."

6. LUA, the mute maiden, has her name resembling the word "loah" which means "pharynges."

7. TARBIT. the name of the clay fellow, has the same Hebrew grammatical root with "tarbut" that means "culture."

8. CLAM, the name of the kind shepherd, may be read in Hebrew in an inverted way as "melech" ("king").

9. MILGA, the name of Tarbit's wife, means "award" in Hebrew.

Legends from Vamland is a book which has literally changed me as a person, restoring my confidence in the human being's power to overcome his or her own weakness. It has also restored my confidence in the power of words as a means of communication and reinforced my love for literature itself. In my eyes. *Legends from Vamland* is a masterpiece and "the book of my life."

I gratefully acknowledge the patience and encouragement of the distinguished late Baha'i poet Roger White, former editor of *The Baha'i World and Voices Israel*, who read the manuscript and offered suggestions.

Luiza Carol

Legends from Vamland

Ormag, the master of the immortal gods and goddesses called "narts" and "nartesses,"stood in the great hall of Nartazuba — the narts' home in the sky — which was made of fog. Ormag was surrounded then by all the great and small narts...

Legends from Vamland

Preface

Due to the efforts of a great many contemporary scholars, the Vamitic alphabet and the Vamitic language have been researched and translations have been made available. We are now in a position to give the reader an outline of the most important legends in the mythology of Vamland.

Ormag's Mouse
(Prologue in the Sky)

Once upon a time, Ormag, the master of the immortal gods and goddesses called "narts" and "nartesses." stood in the great hall of Nartazuba — the narts home in the sky — which was made of fog. Ormag was surrounded then by all the great and small narts. He was clad in his frost mantle and his greenish-grey eyes looked so gloomy that the narts shivered with fear. They tried to put him in a better mood, but no one succeeded until Pil, the crippled nart of jokes, thought of a way to amuse him: he recommended that Ormag toy with a mortal man the way cats play with mice. Ormag agreed that such a game would be a completely new and pleasant entertainment for him and, besides, it would teach a lesson to all mankind about the supremacy of narts over mortals.

"And who is the man you have chosen to be my plaything?" asked Ormag.

"His name is Vam and he lives near the Big Sea, master" replied Pil.

Part I: The Burnt-Hearted Man
Chapter 1: "Aspapur Ormag ruc u Vam"

On the shore of the Big Sea there lived a dark-haired fisherman called Vam. He used to draw fish from the sea and sell them to the rich people in the city of Zinu. One afternoon when he had finished his work, he rested on a black rock on the sea shore, listening to the voices of the waves. And suddenly, the rock which had stood still for thousands of years, scampered away and went out to sea. A strange power seemed to tie the fellow to the rock with invisible ropes. Of course. Vam didn't know that the rock was pushed by Ormag and that he was tied up by Zubala, the nartess of night and magic. Great was his wonder when he found himself sailing with the black rock further and further... until, when night fell, he reached an unknown island covered by greenish-grey fog. There was a greenish-grey city on the island and it was surrounded by a greenish-grey wall. A strange old man with cold greenish-grey eyes courteously invited him

...suddenly, the rock which had stood still for thousands of years, scampered away and went out to sea. A strange power seemed to tie the fellow to the rock with invisible ropes...

to enter the city, but after a while the old man disappeared and Vam wandered alone in the darkness along the streets of the forsaken city with greenish-grey empty houses. At last he saw a light and got closer to it. The light was spread by a huge golden bell which hung in the middle of a square. There was a beautiful maiden in the square and she asked Vam. who seemed an agreeable fellow, to pull the bell. She had a strange, sad voice and as she spoke a long forgotten hope seemed to kindle in her dark eyes. Vam pulled the bell and its long knell hovered over the silence of the vacant city. The bell descended as the fellow pulled and it stood glittering in the middle of the square. The maiden asked Vam to open a golden door in the wall of the bell and when he did so his finger as it was pricked by a golden lock. Then the old man who had invited Vam into the city emerged from the golden bell. But now he was wearing the frost mantle and Vam could sec that the clothes under the mantle were made of "slam" — the precious golden fur-like tissue which only the great narts were allowed to wear. The startled fisherman could also see in the old man's right hand the terrifying royal symbol, the great bone-axe!

"Ormag!" whispered Vam in amazement, stepping back.

"It was the tongue of the golden bell" said Ormag. Then the king of the narts told the fellow about his long dispute with Dumvur, the nart of the sea, concerning that island with the Greenish-Grey City. Dumvur claimed the island was his own because it was the sea

Then the old man who had invited Vam into the city emerged from the golden bell. But now he was wearing the frost mantle...

which gave birth to that land, while Ormag insisted that he was a king and was allowed to take away anything he wished from anybody.

"What's your opinion about it, Vam?" he asked suddenly.

"I think that anything which is born by the sea belongs to Dumvur" replied the fellow. But Ormag burst out laughing and then Dumvur himself appeared in the square. He was as green as the sea. with water oozing down his beard and hair and down his clothes which were made of sea-grass and pearls, up to the green scales on his feet which made up a sort of strange shoes. When he saw the drop of Vam's blood tricking down the golden lock. Dumvur went mad with anger and shouted to Vam:

"You'll pay for that, wretched mortal creature!"

Then immediately he vanished into the sea whose water billowed and roared with a threatening surge.

Vam couldn't understand anything that had transpired. but Ormag was very pleased and enjoyed the fellow's embarrassment. Splitting his sides with laughter, he explained that there had been an agreement between himself and Dumvur. According to that agreement. the island would have belonged to Ormag if a man had shed his blood in order to make Ormag's voice sound into the city and cover the voice of the sea which was Dumvur's voice. Vam had just done that very thing, unwittingly, and thus made a strong enemy of Dumvur. "You deserve a reward, Vam "said Ormag between fits of laughter, "and your reward will be Una, the maiden in the Greenish-Grey City."

Then Ormag, still laughing, vanished into the fogs of Nartazuha, while his own image modeled in gold appeared inside the golden bell. The bell turned into a golden temple, and from that time forward, the temple's name has been "Ormag's Bell."

Vam remained alone with the beautiful Una (her name meant "one" in the Vamitic language). Vihta, the fume bird of love, sent by Ormag, bit their hearts stronger than it had ever bitten the hearts of other couples and made them fall in love more deeply than anybody had before or since. Vam learned from Una that she was Ormag's daughter, but her father had never loved her. Una's story is the following:

After getting angry with his wife Zubala, Ormag had fallen in love with Arata, the queen of the bird-girls. He had expected her to bear him a son, and had been so disappointed when Arata gave birth to a girl that he had driven away both mother and daughter. Arata's daughter, Una. had been compelled to live in the Greenish-Grey City and Dumvur had seen her there and had fallen in love her because of Vihta's bite. It was for her sake that the nart of the sea had wanted to keep the island for himself. Ormag had promised to change Una's sad fate if the girl could enable him to win the island, and that's what had made her urge Vam to pull the golden bell... But he forgave her for that. There was a secret about Una that Vam didn't know, though it was known to all the narts: Una was doomed

The bell turned into a golden temple, and from that time forward, the temple's name has been "Ormag's Bell." Vam remained alone with the beautiful Una...

to die if she ever left the island, because Ormag didn't bestow immortality on her. Una didn't tell Vam this secret because Arata advised her not to. (Lacking confidence in all men. Arata was somehow afraid that Vam would reject Una if he knew.)

Vam and Una lived together in the forsaken city and their happy love songs made its greenish-grey walls turn red. Since then its name has been changed too, and "The Greenish-Grey City" became "The Red City." Vam and Una had a baby girl in the Red City and her name was Lua. Their happiness made Dumvur more and more angry, and his face grew even greener than before. But he didn't dare to take revenge because he was afraid of Ormag. On the other hand. Vam and Una's happiness displeased Ormag too. as he was bored and wanted his little game to go on. It was Ormag who lost his temper first and sent Pil to Dumvur to inform him that he was free to take his revenge on Vam because the man was no longer under the protection of the king of the narts. So pleased was Dumvur at the good news that he gave Pil a magic black stone as a gift (it was a stone that Zubala had dropped in the sea once). After that, the sly nart of the sea began to speak to Vam in a gentle alluring voice which seemed the voice of the waves. And Vam was enchanted by the voice and listened attentively to it and did what the voice said. "Take Una and Lua away from the island." said the voice, "and bring them at night to the other shore, near the city of Zinu. Create a surprise for them... they have never seen the beauties of the big rich city on the other shore..."

Vam took Una and Lua away when they were both sleeping (Zubala, the nartess of night and magic, was assigned to ensure that their sleep be very deep at that time) and in the morning, when the boat reached the green shore near Zinu, Vam saw that his beloved Una was dead. His grief was so great that he couldn't even cry when Dumvur turned up to enjoy his revenge.

"Don't mock my human pain with your immortal empty eyes..." said Vam to the scaly nart of the sea, and he went away from the shore. He entered an old forest and when Lua began to cry he stopped and called for Una's mother, Arata. To do that, he had to bind his eyes and Lua's with pieces of cloth from his shirt because Arata, like any other bird-girl, would lose her white wings if any mortal gazed at her, and their loss would mean her death. The beautiful Arata came from her city of nests sheltered by trees. She saw her daughter dead and began to cry. Arata had the magic power to see the events of the past, but she couldn't foretell the future. So Vam had no need to explain to her what had occurred. On the contrary, Arata was able to explain to him that it was Ormag's will manifesting itself in everything that happened to Una and himself. "You'll pay for that. Ormag!" said Vam with such force and anger that Arata was terrified. She tried to silence him but she couldn't. Mad with pain and grief. Vam shouted: "I swear that Nartazuba's walls will collapse and you'll regret what you have done, Ormag!"

The beautiful Arata came from her city of nests sheltered by trees. She saw her daughter dead and began to cry...

Ormag's laughter resounded over the wood when he answered that he accepted the challenge. The little game was becoming more and more exciting for the king of the narts... But Vam entrusted Lua to the queen of the bird-girls and then buried Una's body in a stone tomb. The Vamitic religious tradition was to spread a yellow powder over the dead bodies. That powder, the Vamits believed, had a magic effect of oblivion. Without it, the dead were supposed never to find eternal peace and never to enter Mastazuba — the shadow-world of the dead which belonged to Mastara. the cold nartess of death. "Those who enter Mastazuba will never come back," said Vam, "but you will my love, you will!" And he didn't accomplish the ritual.

Vam took a small piece from the stone of Una's tomb and engraved on it the following words: *Aspapur Ormag ruc u Vam* (which meant: "The powerful Ormag is Vam's enemy"). Then he made a hole in the piece of stone and passed a cord through it and fastened it round his neck.

On the long, dangerous roads which awaited Vam, it was this very piece of stone cut from the tomb of his love, which was going to warm his heart, and fill him with courage.

Chapter 2: The Road of Tears

In the foggy palace of Nartazuba, the narts were celebrating Pil's great success with his attempt to divert the fearsome Ormag. In fact all the great narts felt involved in the same "cat-and-mouse" game and enjoyed it. But in the middle of their gaiety, in came Mastara, the cold nartess-of death, and the laughters ceased as even the narts used to shiver at her sight. Mastara was beautiful beyond description. Her face was as white as the foam of the sea and two glittering ear-lids covered her cars, causing her to hear nothing in the whole world but Ormag's voice. Black veils wrapped her tall slender body and from her silver belt was suspended the black seal with which she used to seal the mortals' eyes when they had to pass into her shadow-world. Mastara was furious and cast the black seal at Ormag's feet. "Why do you allow my humiliation?" she asked Ormag in an angry voice and then told him that Vam the mortal dared to disobey her law and didn't spread the yellow powder of oblivion over his wife's dead body. Ormag laughed and assured the nartess of death that everything would be all right and Vam would receive his due punishment. Satisfied by the words, Mastara took back her seal and disappeared in the depths of her gloomy world while the narts resumed their cheerfulness in Nartazuba.

...Meanwhile Vam, the burnt-hearted man, was walking through the wood. The piece of stone cut from the tomb of his Jove was warming his breast and was protecting him. At night. Zubala's crazy daughters came and surrounded Vam. They numbered hundreds, maybe thousands, and Zubala long ago had endowed them with the power to trick men and torment them and cause them to go insane. Zubala's crazy daughters

...in the middle of their gaiety, in came Mastara, the cold nartess of death, and the laughters ceased as even the narts used to shiver at her sight. Mastara was beautiful beyond description....

appeared under Una's shape and they implored Vam to spread the yellow powder of oblivion over her body. They looked with Una's eyes and talked with Una's voice and pretended to endure excruciating in front of the black flames of Mastazuba which couldn't be crossed without the yellow powder of oblivion. One of them came closer to Vam and said: "You are unable to fight the narts Vam, as the hare is unable to fly, as the rock is unable to move..." But Vam replied: "Everything is possible. The hare is able to fly when the eagle snatches it and the rock is able to move when the river drags it along..." Then the crazy daughters of night tried to drive Vam mad, but the burnt-hearted man took the piece of stone in his hand and uttered in a loud voice: *Aspapur Ormag ruc u Vam* ("The powerful Ormag is Vam's enemy") and Zubala's crazy daughters vanished from sight. Then Vam felt that the power of piece of stone was so great that the whole world trembled at the sound of the words engraved on it and uttered by him. Little by little the burnt-hearted man acquired superhuman powers from the piece of stone and became able to have a vision. In his vision he saw the world as it had been before Ormag's rule and before the sun (who was called "Saian the Lion") had started to give light to the earth. In that world there reigned an indescribable peace which seemed to come from the golden-red light of the legendary apples called "maun-apples." Vam found himself in a time when mankind didn't know fear and death, nor envy, cruelty, and despair. He met there an immortal man

Zubala's crazy daughters appeared under Una's shape and they implored Vam to spread the yellow powder of oblivion over her body....

who was a sage and a visionary. The man seemed to float when he came near Vam, clad in golden clothes of "slam." He looked at Vam with his peaceful golden eyes and understood all his problems. Then he advised the burnt-hearted man to talk with the nartess of death. "If you ant your voice to penetrate Mastara's silver ear-lids of silence, you have to transcend Ormag's law and use a power greater than his. You've got a powerful shield. Vam..." but the immortal didn't finish his words when Vam's vision faded away and the burnt-hearted man couldn't hear what that shield was or how he could use it.

Tired by so many experiences, Vam lay on the grass, wondering how he could reach the nartess of death in the shadow-world. As he was lying on his back, looking at the sun's light which was the light of Saian the Lion... an old legend came into his memory and this was the legend:

The Story of the Bright Saian and the Beautiful Mastara

A long time ago. when the powerful Ormag was in love with his wife Zubala. the nartess of night, the whole earth was covered by Zubala's dark mantle, as the light of the day hadn't been brought forth yet. Zubala's eldest daughter, Mastara. received the kingdom of the shadow-world from her father, but as Zubala went on giving birth to hundreds of daughters and no son, Ormag got angry and became very stingy with all his other daughters. The so-called "crazy daughters of night" had nothing else but the power to cheat the mortals and they were living together with their mother in a rich dark palace in the sky, away from the foggy Nartazuba. Unlike all the other narts, Zubala didn't use to receive oblations from the mortals because she didn't feed herself on the smoke which went up from the altars on the earth. The greedy Zubala had received from Ormag a huge flock of goats who gave her golden milk to drink and golden kids to eat. Besides, Zubala used to sprinkle drops of golden milk on her mantle and those were called "stars" by the mortals, while the "moon" was nothing else but Zubala's face.

At that time, here on the earth, the good shepherd Ta was driving to pasture the goats of the king of Zinu on the lawns of the Cuta Mountain. And none of the following would have ever happened if one goat had not given birth to a golden kid one day. Ta and his wife Glana were amazed by the miracle and Ta went to Zinu to show the king the golden creature born to one of his goats. The king of Zinu was very pleased and immediately ordered the golden kid to be cooked for supper. He was so excited that he forgot to make the usual oblations to the narts and the narts got offended. Ormag sent to Zinu his messenger, the bat-winged Birgun, to ask the king to kill the magical goat with his own hands on the narts' altar, just there on the Cuta Mountain. That's why Ta the shepherd didn't return home alone, but accompanied by the frightened king himself and a large royal escort. When he came home he learned that meanwhile a second miracle happened: his wife Glana had given birth to a golden baby boy after drinking a pail of sweet golden milk from the magical goat. Excited and embarrassed, Ta decided to deceive the king and protect the magical goat. He brought another goat to be sacrificed and it happened so that the king and the narts themselves were deceived. After the king and his escort left, the shepherd brought the magical goat into his hut. Warmed by the two people's affection and care, the goat began to speak with human voice. She said she didn't belong to the king of Zinu but to the powerful nartess of night. She said she had been deeply bitten by Vihta (as you realize, Vihta, the fume bird of love, used to have the same power over narts. mortals, and beasts) and then she had tried to protect the fruit of her love from Zubala's greediness. She had succeeded in doing so by hiding herself among earthly goats, but she hadn't been able to protect her kid from the king of Zinu. The goat was very sad, but she promised to ask Vihta to take care of Ta and Glana's son, whose magical birth was due to her golden milk. Then the goat thanked the shepherd for saving her life and vanished into the darkness.

Ta and Glana were very proud of their son and they called him Saian — which meant "Golden Face" in Vamitic. Saian grew up in the shepherd's hut and as time went on he became a very handsome young man. Years on end his parents managed to hide the dazzling light of Saian's body from the narts' eyes by making him wear goat-skin clothes and a goat-skin mask over his face. But one day Glana was attacked by wolves somewhere near the hut and Saian heard his mother shouting for help. He rushed out of the hut to help her and he had no time to cover all his golden body. Ormag saw an unusual light on the Cuta Mountain for a few moments and sent his messenger Birgun to spy upon that place. The bat-winged nart Birgun did the job very quickly and the narts learned that they had been deceived by Ta. Ormag was amazed at the shepherd's impudence. He decided that Ta deserved a most terrible punishment and that's why he sent Mastara to close Saian's eyes with her black seal. But, as you might remember. Ta and Glana's son was protected by the fume bird of love. The beautiful Mastara came in Ta's hut and she saw Saian without his goat-skin clothes and his goat-skin mask. Vihta bit her heart so deeply that the nartess couldn't take out her eyes from the golden young man. Then Vihta bit Saian's heart and the two people began to whisper love words to each other (as Mastara hadn't yet been deafened). Mastara took Saian in her silver carriage pulled by nine black-winged beasts. The carriage passed through the black gate of Mastazuba and over the black flames surrounding it. Mastara and Saian came to live in the depths of the shadow-world in Mastara's palace of black stone and glittering silver. They were both happy and Saian's body spread an unusual light over the formerly gloomy Mastazuba. The formerly silent palace now became full of their love songs. Mastara and Saian had a son whom they called Cadumal, and the boy had black eyes like his mothers and golden hands like his father's. Mastara's heart was very much changed by her love for Saian and Cadumal. More and more seldom she accepted to quit her family and only when old people got fed up with life and called for her, would she come on the earth to close their eyes with her black seal. It's said that no child during that time and mankind got stronger and stronger and people began to forget their usual fear and respect for the narts. Fewer and fewer oblations sent their spirals of smoke towards the sky and the narts of Nartazuba who got fed only on those wisps of smoke became weaker and weaker, until one day they all came to Ormag and asked him to go and see what was transpiring far away in depths of Mastazuba.

It was the first time that the powerful Ormag ventured to pay a visit to his proud daughter Mastara. He opened the stone gate of Mastazuba by touching it with the bone-axe of power and then he pointed with the axe at the black flames and said: "I'm Ormag and my name is fear!" The black flames parted to let him pass. Ormag went on over the black slabs polished by the steps of millions of shadows. An uncommon light suffused the place and Ormag could see the crowds of shadows of men, woman, and children cramming in their caves, raising towards him shadows of beseeching arms, uttering shadows of prayers with shadows of words. Outside the caves he could see shadows of trees, shadows of grass, shadows of animals, while in the air shadows of birds were flying towards shadows of nests. At last Ormag reached Mastara's palace and he realized that the strange light emanated from Saian's body.

Ormag's frost mantle was waving around and his voice was threatening like thunder when he spoke to his daughter. He scolded her for getting married without his approval. He punished her by putting an ice circle round her heart and by making her forget her love and become as cold as a stone. It was then that Ormag shut the nartess's ears with the silver ear-lids of silence and since then Mastara could hear nothing but Ormag's voice which she obeyed. As for Saian. the king of the narts decided to turn him into a golden immortal lion whom Mastara couldn't recognize. Ormag ordered Saian to walk each day on the sky and give to the earth the light which would be called "day" and then come back to give light to Mastazuba during the time which would be called "night." Ormag didn't wipe away Saian's memory because he wanted his punishment to be more cruel. Mastara had to unlock Saian's cave every morning to send him away on the sky, and every evening she had to lock him again in his cave. The golden lion endured excruciating pains because his former wife forgot everything about him, but he was powerless against Ormag's will. As for Cadumal, son of Mastara and Saian, Ormag was quite generous with him and bestowed immortality on him, making him become a nart. Ormag touched his grandson's lips with the bone-axe of power and decided that Cadumal was

As for Saian, the king of the narts decided to turn him into a golden immortal lion whom Mastara couldn't recognize. Ormag ordered Saian to walk each day on the sky and give to the earth the light which would be called "day" and then come back to give light to Mastazuba during the time which would be called "night."

to be the nart of sleep and his lips henceforth were going to blow waves of sleep over mankind. Since that
time, the mortals have had to spend almost half of
their short lives under the power of Mastara and
Saian's son.

Since then the mortals' prayers have been unable
to reach Mastara's deaf ears and nobody has been able
to warm her icy heart.

And since then the smoke of the oblations offered
on the earth have never ceased to feet the insatiable
narts...

"...Since then..." sighed Vam. the burnt-hearted
man. As he lay on his back, looking at the golden lion
Saian, the piece of stone warmed his heart when he
shouted towards the sky:

"Hey you, golden Saian! Would you help somebody who is Ormag's victim just as you are? Would
you lead me to the shadow-world, please?"

Then the sun (the lion's golden head) seemed to
stop in his way and something like a fiery snake came
down to the earth and Vam understood that was Saian's
tail. Vam climbed up Saian's tail as if it were the rope
of a most miraculous ship and the air of the heights
made him feel almost as free and bold as he had felt
when he was in the world of the past with the immoral
sage, before Ormag's rule. Pil, the crippled nart of
jokes, tried to put Ormag on his guard by advising him
to end the game because it might become dangerous.
But the powerful king of the narts was too fascinated

by the "cat-and-mouse" game and didn't want to stop it yet. He laughed with scorn at Pil's warning and waited to see what would happen.

Vam climbed on the golden lion's back and Saian brought him to Mastazuba. They passed the stone gate and stopped in front of the black flames where poor Una's shadow was tortured. She couldn't come back, nor could she pass through the flames because of her live memories. But although she had no body and Vam couldn't touch her, although her eyes were shut and sealed, she still could recognize Vam's voice and could talk to him. "I'll accept whatever come to me through you, Vam" she told him, and those were the very words she had told him on the earth. There they stood, a man and a shadow, before the black flames of Mastazuba, and they were talking about Lua, about Arata, about the living human world which they carried there in their live memories. Then both of them mounted the lion and were brought in front of the cold nartess Mastara. It was at that moment that a light kindled in Vam's mind and he suddenly understood what the source of his power was. and what that magical shield was which the sage had been talking about: it was the piece of stone cut from the tomb of his love. When he understood that, he took it in his hands and broke the silence of Mastazuba by uttering the words: *Aspapur Ormag ruc u Vam* ("The powerful Ormag is Vam's enemy").

For hundreds of years no other words but Ormag's had passed through Mastara's silver ear-lids, and the stone-hearted nartess shivered when she suddenly heard a mortal's voice. Vam talked to her about Saian and Cadumal and his words melted away the icy circle round Mastara's heart. The nartess remembered her lost love and knelt down and kissed the lion's head.

Although they had been persecuted by the narts, Vam and Una were deeply moved by the nartess's sorrow. Mastara promised to fulfil any wish which Vam might make, and the burnt-hearted man asked her to return Una to life. Mastara hesitated, as she remembered that she herself had asked Ormag to punish Vam. But any promise was engraved on a board by Taruna, the nartess of justice whose handwriting couldn't be erased save with Ormag's approval. So Mastara had to keep her promise and she unsealed Una's eyes. At the same moment Una's shadow vanished as the real Una came to life on the earth. Mastara lent Vam her own silver carriage and immediately the nine mewing black beasts brought Vam to Una's tomb. Vam removed the stone which covered the tomb and Una got up and embraced him. They had a joyous and magnificent moment of peace and happiness, after which the air trembled at Ormag's laugh and the powerful king of the narts came down, clad in his frost mantle. He hatefully blew over Una and made her fall on the grass, but Vam was ready to fight. He took the piece of stone in his hand and uttered the words: *Aspapur Ormag ruc u Vam* ("The powerful Ormag is Vam's enemy") and the whole world trembled at those words while the narts and nartesses of Nartazuba turned pale.

Ormag tried to strike Vam with the bone-axe of power, but Vam was quicker and stopped his arm. Vam's fingers were hurt in the fight, but the axe fell down and he put his foot on it. When Vam did that, there was such an earthquake that even the foggy walls of Narta-zuba trembled and the narts and nartesses fell from their chairs and began to whimper. Ormag stepped back and tried to scare Vam. "I'm Ormag and my name is fear!" he shouted, but his words had no power over Vam who was already stronger than Ormag. Quietly, Vam said again: *Aspapur Ormag ruc u Vam* ("The powerful Ormag is Vam's enemy") and as quick as lightning he took the axe and struck Ormag's right shoulder causing him to fall on the earth. Another earthquake, stronger than the former ones, made the houses of Zinu collapse and the foggy walls of Narta-zuba began to disintegrate. The narts came down and surrounded Vam while the nartesses took Ormag away in Nartazuba. But Vam grew stronger and stronger with the bone-axe in his hand and it was Pil who managed to stop him. Pil asked for peace and said: "What more can you want, Vam? Haven't you got everything you fought for? You have defeated Ormag, made Nartazuba's walls disintegrate, and caused the narts and the nartesses to repent for hurting you. Isn't it enough? What else do you want? Why don't you give us back the bone-axe now and go in peace wherever you want? Let's make peace, Vam!"

"Peace!" said Ramal, the nart of song.

"Peace!" said Dumvur squeezing his wet beard.

Vam said again: "Aspapur Ormag ruc u Vam" ("The powerful Ormag is Vam's enemy") and as quick as lightning he took the axe and struck Ormag's right shoulder causing him to fall on the earth....

"Peace!" mumbled Gurz, the nart of war.

And then Una herself recovered and whispered tenderly: "Peace. Vam!" The burnt-hearted man hesitated. then he bent his head with a sigh and said one word: "OK" and that one word was going to decide his fate. He gave away the bone-axe of power to Gurz and... that very moment all the narts attacked Vam together and overpowered him. The narts bound Vam and Una in Gurz's brass chains and took them to Nartazuba throwing them at Ormag's feet. Ormag was gloomier than ever while he stood on his fog-throne, having his shoulder treated by Zubala's magic. When he took the bone-axe, he noticed it had acquired a long split as a result of the fall and he understood that the end of his reign had begun. But he didn't say anything about that to the narts and nartesses. He snatched the piece of stone from Vam's breast and the burnt-hearted man shouted:

"Deceptive narts. where is your is promise of peace?"

"For us the peace, you stupid oaf!" replied Pil and the narts laughed. Ormag decided upon a most cruel punishment for the two rebellious mortals. He said: "Take them and bind them at both sides of Nartazuba's gate. I bestow immortality on them because I want them to suffer for ever in front of my eyes and remind me for ever that I have to keep tight control over the mortals for the sake of the narts' immortal glory."

The narts quickly accomplished their king's orders and then Ormag hid Vam's piece of stone somewhere in the darkness, at the bottom of the earth, hoping that nobody would ever find it.

But the end this story is the beginning of a new one, because Vam and Una had a daughter and she was still alive...

Part II: Blindfolded Lua
Chapter 1: Ormag's Hate

Far away, near the quick waters of the river Sata, there stood the flint trunks of the tall mythical trees called "caru trees." High in the air, in the big crowns of the trees, there lay the City of Nests in which the bird-girls lived. Each caru-tree sheltered a big nest pro- vided with a white down lining inside, but there were neither streets nor stairs in that city because the bird- girls were transported through the air by their white wings. In the middle of the city, there lay the biggest and whitest nest called "the palace-nest" in which Arata, the queen of the bird-girls dwelt. Such was the place where Vam and Una's daughter Lua had to spend her childhood, carried from one nest to another by the beautiful bird-girls. The bird-girls loved and protected Arata's wingless grand daughter. Lua's eyes were bound all the time because she was a mortal and the look of her eyes would have killed her grand mother and all the other bird-girls. Compelled to live in the darkness, the blindfolded Lua listened to the sounds of the water

High in the air, in the big crowns of the trees, there lay the City of Nests in which the bird-girls lived....

and the wind, the leaves of the trees, and the songs of the bird-girls, waiting for the time when she would be grown-up and leave the City of Nests. Then she would be allowed to unbind her eyes and then the water, the trees, the grass, the people around her would have shapes and colors... Until that time came. Lua used to sing wordless songs and her voice became stronger and stronger as the years passed, while her songs more and more melodious. She was a wonderful tall teenager when her magical voice began to resound far away in the distance and even the dwellers of Zinu could hear it, floating musically upon the air. The king of Zinu used to climb on the flat roof of his palace in order to catch as well as he could the sounds of Lua's lyrical voice. One day he promised a golden fiddle and a silver flute to anybody who could unveil for him the secret of the magical voice. Then an envious fiddler-apprentice had a wicked thought. He went to the Red City and reached the golden temple called "Ormag's Bell." He found there many priests clad in greenish-grey mantles, as the place was a sanctuary now. The fiddler-apprentice sacrificed a black hen and a black buffalo, burned their bowels on Ormag's altar, and gave their meat to the priests. After that, the golden statue of Ormag began to talk to him and advised him to take a black feather from the hen and a black piece of skin from the buffalo because those two things would be of great help to him. The fiddler-apprentice thanked the nart and obeyed his orders. When he blew upon the black feather, it began to fly and it lead him to the

City of Nests which he reached by night. The bird-girls had flown away as they always did each evening, and Lua was left alone singing in the palace-nest. The sly fiddler-apprentice managed to come near her and persuaded her to unbind her eyes. Lua was flustered by the great shock when her eyes opened and began to accommodate to shapes under Zubala's cheating face (which was the moon). The tree, the river, the fellow near her, all the voices which she had heard until then in the darkness, began to turn into shapes before her gaze... She grew giddy and put her hands over her eyes. At that moment Ormag, who was watching everything from his fog-throne in Nartazuba, decided to interfere and whispered an order to Pil who rushed to accomplish it. Pil climbed the golden tower where Gorc, the sky-rooster, was dozing as usual, waiting for the time to announce the dawn. Pil awakened the rooster and made him blow three time the silver trump of dawn... and made him blow three time with the silver trump of dawn... and at the same time Saian the sun climbed out from the depths of Mastazuba to begin his daily walk across the sky. Lua took out her hands from over her eyes an all the colors of the world in all their splendor invaded her senses, painfully. Billows of colors were striking her unaccustomed eyes, when the air trembled as the bird-girls flew home. Unwittingly. Lua looked up and her eyes met Arata's face. The queen fell down like an arrowed swan and her detached white wings folded over her prone body. Then the same thing happened to a second bird-girl who was looked upon by the fiddler-apprentice. All the other bird-girls hid away in panic and their terrified shouts made Lua understand what she had done. Horrified, she stood at the root of the caru-tree, looking for the first time at the face of her dying grand mother.

"It's not your fault" Arata said. "Our family is haunted by Ormag's hate..." And Lua kissed her while Mastara turned up briefly, only to seal the eyes of the two stricken bird-girls. Then Lua wept and spread the yellow powder of oblivion over the two bodies and buried them in the two graves dug by the fiddler-apprentice, while all the bird-girls in the city were crying in the caru-trees, hidden in their nests. After the funeral, the fiddler-apprentice asked Lua to come with him. Lua refused because she didn't trust the fellow who had made her unbind her eyes and kill the being she had loved best in her life. But the fiddler-apprentice forced her to come. He waved the black piece of buffalo-skin and immediately it turned into a black tent which enclosed both of them in it and flew with them until it alighted on the flat roof of the palace in Zinu. The king happened to be there in the midst of a party with his royal musicians. All of them were amazed when Lua emerged from the tent with her face looking white and cold like Mastara's, and with no other clothes but her own long black hair. The king of Zinu rewarded the fiddler-apprentice with a golden fiddle and a silver flute for bringing the singer to him. Then he ordered a woman-slave to dress her up in royal garments, with a white gown and a marten-fur. And then... he ordered Lua to sing and divert him.

Slowly and in silence, Lua looked at the king's red face, at the envious royal musicians, and at last her gaze fell on the face of the fiddler-apprentice. Then Lua raised her head, closed her eyes and began to sing. Her song was wordless like the songs of the water and the wind, but there was such an anguish, such a wild despair, such an anger in her voice, that the king cowered in his chair, the musicians were agape and the women-slave cried unconsciously. Lua's song resounded throughout the whole city of Zinu, then became stronger and stronger and began to mount to the sky. Zubala tried to stop it by making a magical sign with her fingers, but the song was stronger that the power of her magic. Little by little. Lua's song conquered the hall of Nartazuba and although it was wordless, all the narts and nartesses could hear its unuttered message like an echo in their hearts, and this was the message: "The powerful Ormag is Lua's enemy." Lua's song grew louder and louder, Nartazuba's walls began to disintegrate and Una and Vam began to gain strength and to struggle with the chains that bound them at the gate of the narts' pal- ace. *Aspapur Ormag ruc u Vam* ("The powerful Ormag is Vam's enemy") shouted Vam, the burnt-hearted man, and his voice made Nartazuba tremble and the narts grow weaker. Ormag had an impulse to strike the rebellious Lua with the bone-axe of power, but he remembered that the bone was split and didn't dare to use it.

And Lua went on singing. Like billows of anger her voice surged through the narts' palace.

"I'm Ormag and my name is fear!" shouted Ormag. but his words were drowned out by the victorious song. Vam broke a link of his chains and got one arm free. *Aspapur Ormag ruc u Vam* ("The powerful Ormag is Vam's enemy") shouted Vam, showing his fist to the weakened narts.

At that moment Pil began to black-mail Ormag. "I can make them shut up if you give me the bone-axe of power just for one month a year" whispered Pil. But Ormag became offended and refused to give the royal power to the crippled nart of jokes. He asked Birgun to call Mastara, but Birgun's bat-wings were trembling and he couldn't fly.

And Lua continued her singing. Nartazuba's walls were melting away little by little under the waves of her song. "Shoot an arrow, Gurz!" ordered Ormag. But the nart of war was weakened and Vam's arm snatched his arrow-quiver and threw it down into the Big Sea. The huge waves made Dumvur come out in anger from the bottom of the sea, but Lua's song frightened him, too, and the nart of the sea returned hastily to his palace. "One month a year," whispered Pil again in Ormag's ears, and all the narts and nartesses knelt at Ormag's feet and begged him to accept. Ormag was too weak to stand up and his fog-throne was already trembling. "OK" he said.

Pil rushed to earth and arrived at the roof of the palace of Zinu. "Look here, dark-haired singer!" said

Pil. His voice interrupted Lua's song. She opened her eyes. She looked at the crippled creature near her who was offering her a black stone. It was the magical black stone which Zubala had accidentally dropped in the sea one day, and which Pil then got from Dumvur. Unthinkingly, Lua took the stone and at the same time Pil disappeared and the stone blew up and splashed indelible black spots on Lua's face. A deep silence spread over the roof of the palace. Embarrassed, the tired old king withdrew into his bed-room and all the royal musicians withdrew speechless. The fiddler-apprentice took his golden fiddle and silver flute and left without looking at Lua.

The black-spotted Lua remained alone on the roof, in the darkness. The crazy daughters of night surrounded her and they took the shape of Arata and looked with Arata's eyes and spoke with Arata's voice.

"You have killed me," said Arata's shadow.

"It's not my fault, it's Ormag who did it," replied Lua.

"You are a liar," said one of Arata's shadows.

"The lie has stained your face!" said another one.

"Surrender to Ormag's power!"

"Surrender to Ormag's power!" shouted the crazy daughters of night in unison, and they looked with Arata's eyes and spoke with Arata's voice.

"Enough!" cried Lua, sobbing desperately. Then she felt a friendly hand caressing her hair and Zubala's daughters vanished. The woman-slave who had dressed

...Unthinkingly, Lua took the stone and at the same time Pil disappeared and the stone blew up and splashed indelible black spots on Lua's face...

her up and who had been crying all the time during her singing, now stood near her. Respectfully, she led Lua to the slaves' room where she soon fell into a troubled but much needed sleep.

Early in the morning, when everybody else was sleeping, Lua thanked the woman-slave and left the palace quietly. She walked along the silent streets towards the gate of Zinu and departed from the city.

Chapter 2: The Contest with Ramal

Lua journeyed on and on, asking for the road to the City of Nests by the river Sata, but nobody could tell her where it lay. She went along the hot sand of the beach, by the speechless sea, where the shells hurt her tired soles. When she fainted with fatigue in front of a hut. she was in a fishers' village called Gargand.

There lived an old witch in that hut and her name was Braa. When she discovered the black-spotted Lua in her exhausted condition, the witch took her into her hut and gave her a magic drink. Then she washed her feet and anointed them with fish-oil. Lua recovered little by little and when her strength returned she related to Braa the strange story of her life. Braa gave her a pot of greenish-grey water, made some magic signs over her closed eyes and bent Lua's head over the pot. In a few seconds Lua saw Una and Vam's lives unfold before her and also Ormag's vile actions against her. She saw everything in her mind, through her closed eyelids. She understood Ormag's hatred for her and the knowledge gave her so much strength that she began to sing again. But this time her song wasn't sad nor was it angry. Lua's wordless song was glorifying mankind and the supremacy of men over the immortal narts. It wasn't an urge to rebellion any more, but the rebellion itself. The fishermen of Gargand came in front of Braa's hut to listen to Lua's song and their wives looked at them and couldn't recognize them. All the fishermen looked like rich princes in the women's eyes and they seemed so strong as to be able to crush Nartazuba's walls with their arms. Horrified, the narts were listening too. This time Ormag whispered an order to Ramal and Ramal rushed to accomplish it. The nart of the song mounted Saian and made the golden lion bring him to the village of Gargand.

When the great nart came down on the earth astride the sun, Lua stopped singing and looked him in the eyes. At that moment the women recognized their husbands who looked like poor fishermen and again all of them knelt down in front of Ramal. The great nart challenged Lua to a contest to be held in the presence of the royal musicians of Zinu, and promised that the winner would take the other one as a slave. Lua agreed to the contest but she didn't want to go to Zinu. She said. "These fishermen of Gargand have listened to me. You may sing here, too, and let them decide between us."

Ramal agreed. He didn't deign to put his feet on the earth but sang from the back of the sun. The nart glorified fear which was the name of Ormag. The people were breathless and their blood seemed to turn to ice water in their veins. They crouched with their forehead against the ground and felt themselves to be small and mean and weak: it was as though they were under a great burden. When the burden seemed almost unbearable to them, Ramal stopped. The villagers remained silent, not daring to look towards the nart astride the dazzling lion. The nart urged them to announce their choice, but they didn't dare to answer. Ramal understood their silence but too well and said disdainfully: "Let's not lose our time here, let us go to Zinu. The royal musicians are the only ones who are able to make a decision."

But Lua didn't want to go. She called for Taruna, the nartess of justice, to come and prove that Ramal's promise had been written on her board. At Lua's call the four-eyed and four-eared Taruna descended to Gargand. She looked as old as Braa. but she was immortal. The gloomy nartess said Lua and Ramal's agreement hadn't been written on her board because it was against Ormag's law. "A mortal has no right to enslave an immortal," she said, "and any agreement that violates Ormag's law has no value." Then Taruna vanished.

"Let's change the agreement," said Ramal. "Let's sing once again in Zinu. and the loser must swear never to sing again."

"Would such an agreement have any value?" asked Lua.

"I swear," said Ramal.

Then Lua agreed. She said farewell to Braa and mounted. Saian by Ramal's side. Saian brought them to Zinu where the contest was to take place in the king's palace, in the presence of the royal musicians. But the royal musicians said they had already listened to Lua once and that was enough. Fawning upon Ramal, they invited him to sing in order to make that day the happiest day of their lives.

Flattered by this. Ramal sang his hymn to fear which was Ormag's name. The king and his court and the royal musicians listened with their foreheads on the floor, delighted to find themselves feeling small and mean and empty. They felt a sort of fearful and anxious expectation and they enjoyed the experience of it. When Ramal finished, they praised the nart beyond limit. Nobody wanted Lua to sing again, and Ramal asked her to keep her promise and swear that she would cease singing for ever.

"You way of winning means that you feel defeated," said Lua. but the boldness of her words made the nart turn green with anger and everybody felt embarrassed. It was the fiddler-apprentice who broke the silence, saying: "If the singer refuses to obey, she may be forced to."

The king made a sign and all the royal musicians seized Lua and forced her to kneel before Ramal. Then the hangman was called and he had to cut out Lua's tongue right there, on the spot. Ramal decided to give Lua as a slave to the faithful fiddler-apprentice, and the hangman had to carve on Lua's forehead the traditional sign of enslavement. Ramal left and the fiddler-apprentice took Lua to his home.

The fiddler-apprentice's house was small and untidy. He sat down and said, smiling: "I used to think I'd never be able to sing as beautifully as you... But I'll sing better than you, slave, because you won't sing at all! Go and sweep the floor."

But Lua looked at him speechless and without moving. Her expression made the fellow's cheeks heat as if he had been slapped. He grew angry. He took the silver flute and began to his Lua with it and to shout at her.

But Lua stood upright and went on looking at him without moving. The blows cut into her soft white skin but she didn't step aside: it was as if he wasn't feeling anything. At last the fiddler-apprentice got tired and fell down at Lua's feet, dropping the crushed silver flute. Lua stepped over his body, opened the door, and stepped into the street. The people hurrying by were too busy to pay any attention to the black-spotted slave with ragged royal clothes. She found a hidden place in the city in the valley of the river Ritar. There she sat down, hidden by the willow-trees as she used to be hidden by the caru-trees until only a few days ago. But Lua was another person now...

"The powerful Ormag is the enemy of Vam's people." said Lua in her mind, as she couldn't utter words any more. Her fingers were playing in the clay of the valley. The words in her mind became stronger and stronger: "Vam is Ormag's enemy! I'm Ormag's enemy!"

Her voiceless words had such a tremendous power that the waters of the Ritar stopped and a great miracle happened: for a split second, that place in the valley of the Ritar was exempt from Ormag's law. For a split second. that clay in the valley of the Ritar became holier than the fogs of Nartazuba. And in that split second, the piece of clay in Lua's fingers took the shape of a child. A tear from Lua's eyes fell down on the clay-child an the clay-child began to move and to cry. Amazed, Lua found out she had milk in her breasts and began to feed the child. It was a boy and he looked very sweet and grew amazingly quickly... He was already a nice chubby toddler when Ormag's voice rumbled over the valley, the waters of the Ritar resumed their run, Hudu the wind began to blow and Suvava, the goblin of the yellow-fever, came there sent by the king of the narts. Suvava was inconceivably thin, with a spear-like nose and goggled eyes without eyelashes, and he was clad in a greenish fume. He shot an arrow at the child, but Lua covered the baby with her own body and Suvava's arrow pierced her shoulder. Then Suvava vanished, as he never carried more than one arrow at a time. And Lua got ill and suffered there in the valley of the Ritar, while Ormag enjoyed her agony from his fog throne in Nartazuba. Powerless, Vam and Una had to watch Lua's agony, too. from the two sides of Nartazuba's gate, and that made Ormag's satisfaction even greater.

"I'm Ormag and my name is fear!" he shouted, and all the narts began to sing the hymn to their victorious king:

"Ormag, Ormag, thou art the name of fear,

Thou mak'st the whole earth tremble like a deer:

Ormag, Ormag, thou hav'st the axe of bone,

Thy breast is made of brass, thy fist of stone;

Ormag, Ormag, with thy frost foggy flag,

The holy rider of dark clouds, Ormag!

Thou walk'st in glory, fed on precious smokes

From the oblations of the mortal folks:

Thou art the world's most glorious key and lock:

We feel under thy thunder like a flock:

Oh, please accept thy humble sheep to be

For ever in thy shadow to love thee!"

Meanwhile, on the earth, when Lua had drown her last breath. Mastara came and sealed her eyes. But the end of this story is the beginning of a new one, because Lua had a son and he was still alive.

Part III: Tarbit's Heart

Chapter 1: The End of the Glorious City

There lived in the city of Zinu an old potter called Clam and his wife Asta. Vitha had bitten their hearts in their youth and since then they had treasured the warmth of the root of their lives as if they had buried a gem at the root of a young shoot which grew into a huge tree. But they were childless in spite of all their prayers to the narts.

Asta and Clam were very industrious people and when Asta had to launder the clothes she used to get up early in the morning and she was always the first woman who reached the bank of the Ritar River (as that was the place where all the women of Zinu came to do their washing).

One day she came to the Ritar as usual when all the people of Zinu were asleep and... she heard a baby crying under the willow-trees. She discovered a dead woman-slave with a marten-fur round her shoulders lying near the child. Asta left the laundry in the grass, took the marten-fur and wrapped the baby in it. The baby was a little boy and the warmth made him quiet. Asta rushed home, told Clam everything and showed him the baby.

"Maybe this child is just the answer to all our prayers to the narts," she said. "And maybe this child is the son of a powerful nartess who will protect us as a reward for keeping him," she added.

The potter thought it would be better for the little boy if they kept secret the death of the woman-slave. (He was afraid that the woman's master might claim the boy as his slave.) That's why they both went quickly to the Ritar and buried the woman after spreading the yellow powder of oblivion over her body. Nobody saw them when they did it and they came home as quickly as possible to look after the child whom they called Tarbit.

...And time flew away. Asta and Clam grew even older and Tarbit developed into a handsome tall lad with a marten-fur round his shoulders. He helped the old people who had raised him and he loved them very much. As Clam the potter was already weak, Tarbit used to work alone in the workshop. He shaped the pots, painted them and fired them in the kiln, and then displayed them in front of the house in order to sell them. Clam noticed that the fellow was amazingly skilful with the clay. One day, Clam heard Tarbit speaking slowly as he held a piece of clay in his hands. "Whom are you talking to, son?" he asked.

"To the clay," replied Tarbit.

"And what is the clay saying?" asked Clam.

"It says: Give me an order and I'll obey, as we are alike," replied Tarbit.

But Clam was bewildered.

"Let's see: give the clay an order, son," he said. And Tarbit caressed the piece of clay, telling it: "Turn into a hawk, clay."

And Clam's began to tremble when he saw the piece of clay jerking and a clay-hawk appearing in Tarbit's hands. He became excited and immediately told Asta about the miracle. "Tarbit must have a divine origin. as his hands are working miracles," said Clam. "He's my own son! shouted Asta rushing to embrace Tarbit. But Clam said softly: "He *was* our son!" and two tears fell down his cheeks. Then he began to explain to Tarbit that he and Asta weren't his parents, and told him how they had found him. Asta was sobbing during all this time. Tarbit listened in silence. Then he embraced the two old people and said he would still consider them as his own parents because he loved them and was grateful to them. Clam and Asta took Tarbit to the bank of the Ritar and showed him the place where the woman-slave was buried. Then the old people went home and Tarbit remained alone there. He took in his hand a piece of clay from Lua's tomb. He didn't know that he was watched from the sky by Vam who felt such a pain when he saw Tarbit at his daughter's tomb, that a lightning sprang from his eyes and struck the piece of clay in Tarbit's hand. Tarbit was scared and dropped the piece of clay. When he retrieved it, he saw that the lightning had burnt it and three letters were engraved ion it forming the name VAM. Tarbit returned home with the piece of clay and asked Clam and Asta if they could explain that mystery, but they couldn't. Neither could anybody else in Zinu. Still, Tarbit began to keep with him like a talisman the piece of clay with the mysterious name engraved on it.

...And time flew away. Not far from Zinu there lived a people called "the Agrans." Those Agrans were a people kindred to Vamits. Their country was mostly on the water, as they lived in the delta of a big river. Most of the Agrans were fishermen and they built

He took in his hand a piece of clay from Lua's tomb. He didn't know that he was watched from the sky by Vam who felt such a pain when he saw Tarbit at his daughter's tomb, that a lightning sprang from his eyes and struck the piece of clay in Tarbit's hand....

reed huts and were not accustomed to stone walls and streets. They were particularly dedicated to the cult of Zubala. It was Zubala who incited the Agrans against the Vamits of Zinu. Zubala appeared to the king of Agra in a dream and said: "Oh, king of Agra, how long will you allow the Vamits of Zinu to laugh at the Agrans and despite them? Raise your people against them and I promise to give you the whole city of Zinu with its people and walls, so that your riches will be innumerable." Then Gore the sky-rooster blew the trump of dawn and the king of Agra awoke and told his people about that dream. Zubala didn't tell the real reason which made the narts hate the city of Zinu: Tarbit. Lua's son bred by Asta and Clam, was the reason. It was because of that fellow that the narts decided to destroy Zinu, but of course the king of Agra couldn't have guessed it. He had simply obeyed Zubala's orders when he led his men and encircled the city. But the Agrans were unaccustomed to walls and didn't dare to enter the city by night, although Zubala's magic made the sentinels of Zinu sleep just for that purpose. The Agrans were content to surround the city and wait for the dwellers of Zinu to surrender. The narts were disappointed next morning, when they saw Zinu hadn't been invaded yet. The narts didn't give up the plan to destroy Zinu, but now they decided to punish the Agrans, too, for their unnecessary hesitation. So Ormag began to encourage the dwellers of Zinu against the Agrans, while Zubala encouraged the Agrans and a big war began to delight the eyes of the narts. After the first clash of arms, the priests of Zinu and those of Agra took the old stone knives and dedicated to Gurz the hearts of the first dead enemies from both sides. "Long live Gurz!" shouted the warriors when Gurz's huge shadow appeared on the sky (brought up by the oblations, the nart of war had come to excite the warriors of Zinu and those of Agra). And the war grew even more ferocious.

Tarbit had been on the walls of Zinu since the beginning of the conflict. He had insulted the Agrans like everybody else, he had grown angry and threatened them like everybody else, he had shot arrows at the enemies like everybody else... but now strange feelings began to haunt him. Tarbit had seen old friends (his former playmates in the valley of the Ritar) falling dead from the walls of Zinu, and now he asked himself: "Why? Hadn't they been urged by the narts to fight?" He had seen the bleeding hearts of the enemies under the priests' knives and now he asked himself: "Why? Hadn't they been urged to fight by the cruel narts?" And he felt remorse and guilt for the death he caused, and compassion for the unknown mothers whose sons he might have killed with his arrows. He found there were no more arrows in his quiver, but on the bottom of it his hand felt the piece of clay with the name VAM engraved on it. A strong determination seized Tarbit and he went home. He said to Clam: "Bring me clay from the valley of the Ritar, please!"

Tarbit began to caress the clay and the clay said: "Give me an order and I'll obey, as we are alike."

"Turn into a man, clay, "whispered Tarbit and the clay jerked and turned into a clay-man.

"Give me an order and I'll obey, as we are alike," said the clay-man to Tarbit. Tarbit ordered the clay-man to go to the war and fight and the clay-man obeyed.

More and more clay was brought by old Clam from the valley of the Ritar, and Tarbit worked day and night in the workshop creating more and more clay-man and sending them to the war, until all the live warriors in Zinu could be replaced by clay-men. The people in Zinu were happy and the warriors' mothers blessed Tarbit, but the fellow didn't stop working. He worked and worked until one night he opened the gate of the city. Nobody was there to stop him as all the sentinels had been replaced by his clay-men. Tarbit sent another army of clay-men to the people of Agra to replace the Agran warriors, too.

Next morning, when the war was resumed, the two armies of clay-men were shooting arrows at one another and no human being was hurt. The clay-men looked quite strange with the arrows thrust into their breasts, their foreheads, and their eyes. In fact they looked like funny huge hedgehogs, but they didn't mind their comic appearance, and went on fighting.

"What king of a war is this?" shouted Gurz. All the narts and nartesses felt very offended indeed by the mortals' impudence. "Shoot at the city of Zinu, Gurz!" ordered Ormag, and immediately the nart of war shot one of his ruthless arrows towards Zinu. Nine hundred

...The clay-men looked quite strange with the arrows thrust into their breasts, their foreheads, and their eyes. In fact they looked like funny huge hedgehogs, but they didn't mind their comic appearance, and went on fighting.

and ninety-nine people fell dead on the streets of Zinu, killed by Gurz's sole arrow, and the horrified survivors understood that the death which came from the sky was the narts' punishment. Asta and Clam were among the dead and Tarbit buried the two old people in the valley of the Ritar, near Lua's tomb. (The narts spared Tarbit's life only to keep him for a more cruel and exemplary punishment.)

The king of Zinu made oblations to Ormag and asked the priests the reason for Ormag's anger. The oldest priest spoke: "That's what Ormag says: 'Dwellers of Zinu, you have to punish the man who defied the immortal narts by making clay-men with his own wretched mortal hands. I'm Ormag and my name is fear! I order you to sacrifice Tarbit!'"

The thunder rumbled over Zinu when the priest finished his words and the people were silent as they were torn between fear and sorrow. The warriors whose lives had been saved by Tarbit hesitated to arrest the handsome youth, but the king of Zinu told them: "That man is a traitor! Not only did he defy the narts, but he also sold clay-men to the Agrans and made them fight against his own city!"

The king's slanderous words made the warriors seize Tarbit, but the priests didn't sacrifice him on the altar immediately. They decided that the oblation for the city's redemption hat to be purified and cleansed, so Tarbit had to fast for three days and three nights and only on the fourth day his blood was to be shed on the altar. That's why Tarbit was put into prison, while the warriors went up the walls of Zinu where the clay-men were still fighting and threw them over the walls, breaking them and thus hoping to receive Ormag's forgiveness. But alas! The Agrans were still using the clay-men sent to them by Tarbit, only now they were fighting the flesh-and-blood Vamits of Zinu. And the fight was very unfair indeed...

In the prison. Tarbit was more angry. He understood that the narts were playing with the mortals as if they were marbles. He snatched in his fist the piece of clay with the name VAM engraved on it and he swore: "As long as I live, you won't have peace, narts!"

But the narts of Nartazuba didn't hear Tarbit. as they were busy with the end of the war. They were delighted to watch the plunder of Zinu, the old people killed by the invaders, the woman and children bound and branded with the mark of slavery...

The king of Agra captured the king of Zinu and he swept the floor of the palace with his enemy's beard and washed it with his lips.

Meanwhile, unseen by the narts, Tarbit raised a stone from the floor of the prison and caressed the clay under it. "Give me an order and I'll obey, as we are alike" said the clay.

And Tarbit said: "Turn into an eagle, clay."

A thick smoke was rising from the ruins of the glorious city of Zinu, and the smoke concealed the clay-eagle from the narts' eyes. The eagle flew away through the window of the prison with Tarbit on its back.

Chapter 2: The Balance of the World

A short time after the fall of Zinu, Pil's turn came to reign over the narts and mortals, as he had received from Ormag permission to be a king for one month a year. Ormag used to leave Nartazuba and live in Zubala's palace during that month, as he could not bear to obey somebody else's orders.

The reign of the crippled nart of jokes meant a change in the narts' common way of life, because playful Pil was always inventing some sort of trick, and the narts laughed more than they usually did. On the other hand, Pil's tricks weren't always so pleasant for those who were laughed at... Gurz was one of Pil's favorite targets, because he was both powerful and stupid, and that combination qualified him to be an ideal laughing stock. One day, when the narts were amusing themselves as usual at Gurz's expense (Pil had just hidden his arrows) the fog of Nartazuba began to tremble and a clay-eagle came through the gate of the narts' palace, bearing a man on its back. The narts' joy vanished and the silence was broken by Una's voice when she shouted: "Tarbit!"

"Yes, it's me, Tarbit" said the fellow. "I'm here to call you to account, narts!" And Nartazuba's walls began to disintegrate, as they had done on earlier occa-

...the fog of Nartazuba began to tremble and a clay-eagle came through the gate of the narts' pal- ace, bearing a man on its back....

sions. Pil hesitated to throw the bone-axe of power at Tarbit, because he knew that it was split.

"Help him, Vam!" shouted Una to her enchained husband.

"Vam? Is it your name which is engraved on this piece of clay?" asked Tarbit, with great wonder in his voice.

"You are my grandson, Tarbit" said Vam, struggling with his chains.

At that moment a huge split appeared in one of Nartazuba's walls and the narts saw the endless darkness outside.

"Why are those people enchained?" shouted Tarbit.

"It's long story," whispered Pil "but I'm going to tell it to you, brave young man..."

And Pil tried to appease Tarbit's anger with sweet words. But Una shouted in despair: "Don't believe him, Tarbit! The narts' words are full of deception... Ormag and Dumvur have cheated me and Vam, Ormag and Ramal have cheated your mother Lua, and I feel you will be destroyed by Ormag and Pil!"

Tarbit was bewildered when he heard Una's prophecy, and just then he and his clay-eagle were caught into a trawl. It was Luf, Dumvur's son, the small nart of fishing, who had thrown the trawl and won the narts' admiration for the first time in his life. Pil didn't want to kill a man who was continuing the "cat-and-mouse" game which Ormag had begun with Vam. He thought it was Ormag's right to punish him. So Pil ordered Birgun, the bat-winged messenger, to fly with Tarbit to the bottom of the world and throw him there and let him wait. He also instructed Birgun to destroy the clay-eagle and the dangerous piece of clay with the name VAM engraved on it. Birgun accomplished the orders in a twinkling of an eye. And Nartazuba's walls were reintegrating quickly while Tarbit walked alone through the bare greenish-grey realm at the bottom of the earth. There in the darkness. Tarbit listened to the bare vaults humming and the echoes telling a story. And this is the story:

How Ormag Was Born

Once upon a time the sky and the earth were together and there was one people living both in the sky and on the earth, enjoying the golden-red light of the maun-apples. There was no night, no sleep, no death. There were no narts at all and Vihta alone reigned over the world which seemed like a large garden blooming in splendor and song under the invisible wings of the fume bird. People were not divided into rich, poor and slaves: everybody was rich and free. Their thoughts were so pure and their hearts were so light that they were able to fly whenever they wanted to...

There were many cities in that beautiful world and one of the most glittering was the city with golden palaces and ruby gates called Naat. In that city there was a fair maiden called Dlada. She lived in a golden palace like everybody else, she wore golden clothes of slam like everybody else, she had golden eyes like everybody else... but Vihta itself had painted Dlada's eyebrows with its feather and that's why she shone in beauty like a golden flower... When this story begins, the people of Naat were just celebrating Vihta's holiday in a glade near the city. They were singing and dancing as usual over the crowns of the trees and Vihta was biting the hearts of the maidens and fellows who were to be married that year. At that time Vihta had not yet been subjugated by Ormag and that's why it used to bite only fit pairs and never made two people fall in love with the same person. The young couples came down in the glade hand in hand, and among them Dlada came down with a handsome boy called Fin. But when the last couple had to come down in the glade, something very strange happened: Lip (a crippled fellow who had injured his body in his childhood when he fell out of a window) approached Dlada and took her left hand, though Fin was already holding her right hand. That was very queer indeed. And the more so, because the last maiden, Alabuz, who had to be Lip's partner, came down alone with her heart unbitten by Vihta. Maybe the excitement of the young dancers made the fume bird of love lose its head... anyhow, it was obvious that Vihta made a mistake as it had never done before, and its bite was incurable.

Dlada and Fin kindly asked Lip to retreat and not to spoil their joy. The people told Lip and Alabuz not

...the people of Naat were just celebrating Vihta's holiday in a glade near the city. They were singing and dancing as usual over the crowns of the trees and Vihta was biting the hearts of the maidens and fellows who were to be married that year.

to worry but to wait until next day when the City's Assembly would meet and try to find a solution to their problem. Then all the people of Neat rose in the air, floating towards Vihta's Star (that's what the Vamits used to call the Evening Star where they had to celebrate the oath of love.)

Lip and Alabuz remained alone in the glade — the former mad with pain, the latter mad with shame. They both shared the same lack of confidence in the City's Assembly and talked about finding a solution to their problem by themselves. Then suddenly Bolob the jeweler appeared from behind a tree. He didn't rise into the air with the others because his heart was heavy with envy: the jewel he created for the contest at Vihta's holiday wasn't considered the most beautiful one and the City's Assembly gave the first prize to another jeweler. That's why Bolob resented the City's Assembly. The three of them agreed to meet next morning at the Cold Cave behind Naat and discuss their problems privately before the Assembly's meeting opened.

And indeed they met next day, when Lip brought along another two friends who both had different reasons to resent the City's Assembly: Lamar the musician who was allowed only to beat the drum because the City's Assembly hadn't chosen him among the best musicians of Naat, and Zrug the wrestler who had lost a wrestling contest during Vihta's holiday and thought that the City's Assembly hadn't been fair to him. The five of them entered the dark Cold Cave which led to the mysterious bottom of the earth. Nobody had ever come into that cave before, because of the strange smells coming from its other end... The air in the cave was intoxicating and the five people could hardly breathe. When they finally stopped and sat down, they felt something like a cold greenish-grey fog surrounding them, entering their nostrils and mouths and penetrating their bodies. They felt cold and giddy and when they began to speak they understood that it was somebody else speaking with their mouths.

"From the beginning of the world I'm crawling on the darkest bottom of the earth..." said Zrug.

"...waiting" said Lamar.

"I have no name in the golden-red light..." said Alabuz.

"... but you'll give me a name" said Lip.

"Ormag!" shouted Bolob.

They knew the greenish-grey fog was seizing their hearts and they knew they brought into men's world a mysterious and dangerous power.

Strange feelings began to haunt them for the first time:

"I'll always remain unmarried," thought Alabuz.

"I'll always remain a laughing-stock," thought Lip.

"They'll take away even my drum," thought Lamar.

"Everybody will defeat me," thought Zrug.

"They won't give me any more gold," thought Bolob.

And all five of them knew the power and the name of fear: Ormag. And Ormag spoke with their mouths when they said:

"From now on I'll always be with you..."

"... in you..."

"... and I'll mark your hearts with my seal..."

"... because I'm Ormag..."

"... and my name is fear."

Being inside their minds, Ormag knew all their fears and promised to accomplish their most deep-hidden wishes if they obeyed his orders. Then and there, Alabuz, Lip, Bolob, Lamar, and Zrug swore obedience to Ormag, wrote the oath on the wall of the cave with their own blood and signed it. Then and there, Ormag instructed them what they had to do. And when they came out of the cave, fear came out into men's world. The five of them began to be afraid of the golden-red light of the maun-apples. They were afraid to look straight into other people's eyes because at that time people could read the thoughts in each other's eyes and they were afraid to reveal their thoughts. When the City's Assembly met, Lip and Alabuz were afraid to express their opinions, so they kept silent with their eyes down. The Assembly thought they didn't attach importance to the incident any longer, so they didn't consider it necessary to discuss it at all. But Alabuz, Lip, Bolob, Ramal, and Zrug had fear in their hearts and they obeyed Ormag's orders. Each of them made a stone altar and sacrificed a ram on it and five pillars of smoke rose into the air looking like five silent threat-enings. Day after day they offered oblations to Ormag and the other people of Naat began to feel embarrassed when they happened to meet them. They couldn't understand their curious behavior because nobody had ever made oblations to Ormag or to anybody else until then, but they tolerated their whims which didn't seem dangerous.

One day, Alabuz came to Dlada and talked to her. She said that if Vihta had made one mistake, it might make another one too... it might bite a man's heart for a second time for instance... Alabuz took Dlada's hand and Dlada felt a cold shiver and was seized by fear. A queer thought came to her, that her husband Fin might be bitten by Vihta for a second time and fall in love with another woman. Never had such a thing happened before in the golden-red light of their world, but Ala-buz persuaded Dlada that there was a power which might protect her against such an evil, a power greater than Vihta's, and that power was called Ormag. So Dlada began to make oblations to Ormag also. Little by little, more and more people began to make obla-tions to Ormag, and the eyes of those people changed their color and became greenish-grey. Thoughts couldn't be read in the greenish-grey eyes, but only fear. Ormag's name, was reflected in their irises. Mean-while, Lamar became so afraid that people won't let him sing any more that adopted the habit of singing at all the meetings, while the best musicians of the city had fewer and fewer opportunities. Zrug became so afraid that everybody would defeat him, that he made a habit of quarreling with everybody he met and was wrestling all the time. Bolob developed a queer habit too: he began to gather gold ingots compulsively and store them in his house, because he was afraid he won't receive any more gold to work upon. As for Lip. he began mocking everybody because he was afraid of being laughed at. And more and more pillars of smoke were shadowing the golden-red light of the maun-apples...

...And when Vihta's holiday came again, all the people of Neat had greenish-grey eyes and made obla-tions to Ormag in the glade before celebrating their love. The smoke of their oblations made a huge cloud in the sky and the thunder, which was Ormag's voice, rumbled over people's heads for the first time. A green-ish-grey giant was riding the cloud and the people of Naat knew he was Ormag. He was clad in a frost man-tle, his beard was fluttering like a flag of fog and he clutched in his hand the big bone-axe of power. Some-thing like a heavy burden pressed the people's shoul-ders and since then nobody could ever rise into the air as before. On that day, Ormag called to him Alabuz, Lip, Bolob, Lamar, and Zrug who rose into the air and joined him, because Ormag couldn't rule over the world alone and needed the help of a few faithful peo-ple. The five of them came to live with Ormag in the sky and Ormag invested them with the title of "great narts." He changed their names, too. when he changed their destinies, and reversed the letters of their names:

A greenish-grey giant was riding the cloud and the people of Naat knew he was Ormag. He was clad in a frost mantle, his beard was fluttering like a flag of fog and he clutched in his hand the big bone-axe of power....

Alabuz became Zubala, the great nartess of night: Lip became Pill, the great nart of jokes: Lamar became Ramal, the great nart of music: Zrug became Gurz, the great nart of war: Bolob became the great nart of richness without changing his name (the Vamits thought that greediness had to remain greediness whichever way you read its name). After a while Mastara was born (Ormag and Zubala's first daughter) and she became the great nartess of death. So the number of the great narts was six by now and never grew more than six. When some other people were called by Ormag to help him rule over the earth, they were invested with the lower title of "small narts." For example Dumvur (the nart of the sea) and his son Luf (the nart of fishing), Cadumal (the nart of sleep), Suvava (the goblin-nart of yellow-fever), Birgun (the bat-winged messenger), Gorc (the sky-rooster), Hudu (the wind), and even old Taruna (the nartess of justice) and Zubala's daughters and others were only "small narts" and their power was more limited than the power of the "great narts."

The great narts kept only for themselves the indestructible clothes of slam. The great narts and Ormag and Taruna were the only ones who knew the secret of the oath written with blood on the wall of the Cold Cave. On the smoke of the mortals' oblations the narts were fed and from that smoke they built up Nartauba's walls. All the narts, great or small, retained the ability to fly and remained immortal. Mastara began to seal the eyes of the dwellers of the earth and bring their shadows in Mastazuba, because Ormag wanted the mortal men to be weak and afraid of death. From that time, Vihta, the fume bird of love, was subject to Ormag's power (although the king of the narts was more of less afraid of its bite).

And time went on and people forgot about the opulent old city of Naat with glittering golden palaces and ruby gates, forgot about the time when the sky and the earth were together and the whole world looked golden-red like the golden-red skin of the maun-apples...

***

So Tarbit was alone in the darkness, cast down to the bottom of the earth, and there he understood how the narts came to rule over mankind. His heart shivered with sorrow for the long forgotten city of Naat with golden palaces and ruby gates...

"I was right to hate you, narts!" shouted Tarbit in the darkness, and the power of his words was sufficient to defeat fear, Ormag's name. He walked and walked until he stumbled over something and then he found a hot stone, shining like a live ember, and on the stone he could read the words *Aspapur Ormag ruc u Vam* ("The powerful Ormag is Vam's enemy"). It was the stone cut from Una's tomb and warmed at the breast of the burnt-hearted man, the stone which Ormag had hidden once because he was afraid of its tremendous power. Had Pil known that Vam's stone was there, he wouldn't have sent Tarbit to the bottom of the earth. But nobody knew that but Ormag, and Ormag had thought that nobody would ever come in such a place.

Tarbit put the stone at his breast and understood the whole history of Vam and Lua's fight against Ormag. "The powerful Ormag is Tarbit's enemy," shouted Tarbit and the stone in his hand began to give more and more light like a torch. He walked and walked until he saw red letters written on a rocky wall and by the light of Vam's stone, he could read the oath which the narts had written a long time ago:

> We have written this oath with our own blood in the presence of the powerful Ormag. As long as these words live on the rock we shall be the slaves of our master Ormag. And we are signing with our blood:
>
> Alabuz, Lip, Bolob, Lamar, Zrug.

Tarbit scratched away the letters of the oath with Vam's stone and effaced them. Then he continued walking straight ahead and he knew he was following the footsteps of those who had introduced Ormag into men's world. After a while, Tarbit saw a light and he reached the entrance of the Cold Cave. He enjoyed breathing the fresh air under Saian's light. But when he looked around, he was sad to see the earth overgrown by weeds and foliage covering the ruins of Naat. He knew that the silent hillocks were covering palaces and streets and squares... And Tarbit went to the biggest hillock and caressed the earth whispering: "Get away, clay." The hillock quivered and the clay rose and

Tarbit put the stone at his breast and understood the whole history of Vam and Lua's fight against Ormag. "The powerful Ormag is Tarbit's enemy," shouted Tarbit and the stone in his hand began to give more and more light like a torch....

drifted away and Tarbit had before him the most beautiful palace of Naat, where the maiden Dlada had once lived. The gold and the rubies had been stolen by people in whose hearts Bolob had put his own hunger for gold and precious stones: but the walls and the furniture remained almost untouched and Tarbit walked through the room until he found a bed and had a rest. Cadumal blew over his tired eyes and he slept for one day and one night...

Meanwhile, the rebellion seized Nartazuba. Pil's month of reign was over and Ormag came back, but the crippled nart of joke refused to leave the throne. The great narts were fed up with Ormag's tyranny and started to encourage Pil. Taruna said that the great narts' oath had been erased from the wall of the Cold Cave and therefore it had been erased from her board too. But Ormag got angry and took the bone-axe from Pil by force and sat himself on the fog throne roaring: "I'm Ormag and my name is fear!" And all the narts knelt down trembling.

Still, there was a hope kindled in the narts' hearts to get rid of Ormag and that's why they decided to hide Tarbit from Ormag's anger. They thought they wold be able to use the fellow against their king. So the narts covered Naat with a thick cloud, and Tarbit could sleep quietly in the old palace. When he got up he felt quite lonely and sad. He found a pair of clothes of slam in a stone wardrobe and he took out his martenfur and put on one of them. He enjoyed the indestructible golden fur, soft and light like down. He

Tarbit went to the biggest hillock and caressed the earth whispering: "Get away, clay." The hillock quivered and the clay rose and drifted away and Tarbit had before him the most beautiful palace of Naat, where the maiden Dlada had once lived.

took the other clothe in his hand and went out of the palace where he began to caress the clay and the clay said: "Give me an order and I'll obey, as we are alike." Then Tarbit whispered:

"Turn into a maiden, clay,

as beautiful as a fay,

gracious and bold and black-eyed:

turn into a perfect bride."

A beautiful maiden came to life in Tarbit's hands and he clad in the slam clothes and touched her eyes and her breast with Vam's stone. He called the maiden Milga and Vihta came to unite them.

Now Tarbit wasn't alone any more. He had a courageous, intelligent wife and he had plenty of time to talk to her about his fight against the narts. And Milga said: "The narts are powerful, Tarbit, you can't fight them alone. You need other people's help."

Tarbit agreed with the wisdom of what Milga had said. One day he began to ask the hillocks of clay one by one to uncover the old palace of Naat. The hillocks looked like huge eggs which were knocked from within by huge stone chicks with stone beaks. In a few hours the whole city of Naat came out from under the earth. Then Tarbit took Milga outside the city, where he gathered all the clay he had taken from over the palaces, the streets, and the squares. He caressed the clay and began to make clay-fellows while Milga followed his example and began to make clay-maidens. They touched their clay-people's eyes and breasts with Vam's stone and they acquired life. All of them were beautiful and strong and bold and each of them was different. When they made enough dwellers for the whole city, all of them opened their mouths for the first time and shouted: "The powerful Ormag is the enemy of Vam's people!" And their voices made the walls of the palaces cover themselves with gold and the gates cover themselves with rubies. Wistaria sprang from the earth with its violet flowers and along the streets appeared big trees with glittering maun-apples. Everything was as beautiful as in old times, and Vihta came to unite the young people's hearts.

Tarbit and Milga weren't alone now and they were happy. But during the night, the crippled nart of jokes came into Tarbit's dream. "Forget the incident between us," said Pil. "You have effaced the narts' oath from the rocky wall and now you deserve a reward. You and me must be together in our common fight against Ormag. Ask me anything you need to defeat Ormag."

"I need nothing," said Tarbit. But Pil smiled saying: "You don't trust the narts' words, do you? Well, I promise to fulfil three wishes for you. There time you'll have the opportunity to see that Pil is your friend."

After that, Tarbit got up and told Milga his dream. Milga said:

"We are many now in Naat and we can defeat Ormag with or without the narts' help. What would you like to start with?"

Wistaria sprang from the earth with its violet flowers and along the streets appeared big trees with glittering maun-apples. Everything was as beautiful as in old times, and Vihta came to unite the young people's hearts.

"I'd like to reach Panca the giant," said Tarbit.

But as soon as he uttered the words he found himself in front of Panca the giant. Panca was an enormous giant who kept in his hands the balance of the world. He took care that the pan of the sky looked heavier than the pan of the earth and thus he favoured the narts' luck over men's. When he reached Panca, Tarbit uttered his second wish: "I want to talk to Panca and ask him keep the balance straight, so that men have a fair chance against the narts."

But Pil got scared when he heard Tarbit's second wish. Pil would have liked to defeat Ormag only to replace him and inherit his whole power. He couldn't accept to diminish the narts' power. So he abandoned Tarbit there, being convinced that the fellow would never be able to talk to Panca the giant.

Tarbit felt that he was abandoned but he didn't give up. He said aloud in the desert realm: "The powerful Ormag is the enemy of Vam's people!" and he acquired superhuman powers which enabled him to climb on Panca's shoulder. There was a cold strange light striking Tarbit's eyes painfully, as there was no night, no shadow, no cloud on that realm. And even Hudu the wind couldn't reach that place. In that light the fellow could see Panca's huge face, immobile like eternity. Panca's dark eye seemed a bottomless sea in which no thought could be read. And when Tarbit looked down he could see far, far away, the balance of the world with the pan of the earth and the pan of the sky, and his heart shrank with longing for the city of

Naat with golden palaces and ruby gates where Milga was waiting.

"Father of the balance!" shouted Tarbit "Listen to a man who comes from the pan of the earth!" But Panca didn't move and Tarbit understood that his voice couldn't reach the giant's ears. Then he untied Vam's stone from round his neck and the stone flew up to Panca's eye which it touched. A huge eyelid covered the eye in wonder and a huge glistening globe fell from the eye. Tarbit understood that it was a tear and he saw his own image reflected in Panca's tear. Then Vam's stone flew into Panca's ear and came back into Tarbit's palm. The giant's lips moved and Tarbit heard him saying: "Oh Tarbit, what's the use of my eyes as huge as seas if I can't see with them the image of pain? As you people don't know anything about the hearts of the ants, so I don't know anything about people's tears... I can see the earth and the sky but I can't see what happens on the earth, nor in the sky!"

Tarbit understood that the stone made Panca understand everything he wanted to tell him. So he added: "Father of the balance, you give priority to the pan of the sky and that's why men know injustice from the moment they are born."

Panca sighed and when he spoke again there was great sorrow in his words: "Oh Tarbit, it's too late for regrets and no tears of today can eradicate one single tear of yesterday... but listen to my story and then judge with your own heart."

And Tarbit listened in amazement to:

In that light the fellow could see Panca's huge face, immobile like eternity.... And when Tarbit looked down he could see far, far away, the balance of the world with the pan of the earth and the pan of the sky, and his heart shrank with longing for the city of Naat...

The Story of Panca the Giant

A long, long way off, beyond all charted ways, there lies my country of flint, Tarbit. It's called Gudulland. and it's inhabited by giant Guduls and Gudulesses. They are very tall people, much taller than me — in fact I myself am among the shortest Guduls of that country and my people used to tease me for that: but I didn't mind.

I didn't like that bare country of flint, Tarbit, and I didn't get along with its people. I didn't enjoy the Guduls' parties where they competed for the honour to be among the best drinkers of "tev" (that "tev" by the way is a juice which they used to prepare from the seeds of a Gudulic plant, and those seeds are as tiny as a big pumpkin of the earth). I didn't enjoy the Guduls' hunting parties, when they used to beat up some poor unfortunate "haf" (a "haf" is little hopeless creature resembling a stag, not much bigger than the biggest mountain of the earth). Nor did I enjoy the Guduls' wrestling matches, nor their meetings with their vulgar laughters and jests. Days on end I used to carve and polish the grey walls of flint, trying to change a little the gloomy aspect of Gudulland. But I couldn't do much. So bored I was by the lack of beautiful in Gudulland, that one day I decided to go to one the Guduls' vulgar parties because at least they used to be in good mood there. I remember the beautiful sunset of that evening, the reddish shadow over my flint country... The sunset was the only beautiful sight of Gudulland, and whenever I contemplated it I felt sorry for the poor rude Guduls who couldn't even dream of a more refined pleasure than their horrible tev.

When I joined the party it was already late and the Guduls and Gudulesses were a little tipsy already. They were throwing away empty barrels of stone and they enjoyed the noise the barrels made when they broke to pieces. The moment they saw me they began to mock me. "Bring some tev for little Panca!" some of them began to roar and they forced me to drink more than I wanted to. I was quite unaccustomed to that damned tev and I felt as if breaking myself into picces first. But after a while I got queerly bold and lost control over my words. I began to speak aloud: "Sillier than the hafs you are and much uglier than them! Your life is silly and ugly! Why aren't you fed up with yourselves?"

And I went on insulting the Guduls and the Gudulesses who shouted at me and became more and more angry, until they decided to punish me. The dwellers of Gdulland are immoral so they can't kill each other, but they have a most cruel punishment for those who make them angry: they shut them alone in stone barrels and throw them into the endless space. That's what they've done to me.

I'm shut for ever in a stone barrel. Tarbit, and if your eyes can't see its walls, it's because you are so small and the barrel is so big. I have no idea how long it is since I've begun my eternal fall, but I know I have no chance to get away from here...

...Yes, they've shut me for ever in a stone prison, but they haven't defeated me. I was haunted by my old aspiration from Gudulland, the wish to improve life and make it more beautiful. I had a knife in my pocket and I began to scratch the walls of the barrel and chew the chips of stone with my teeth. In the end I made a sort of flour of stone and I could model with it a sort of cake which you now call "earth." I did it as beautiful as I could and when I looked at it I suddenly felt sorry for my lost flint country which I hadn't been able to improve and make more beautiful. I felt so sorry that I began to cry and my tears fell on the cake of the earth and they became rivers and seas. When I ceased crying, my toy was more beautiful, but somehow barren. I found a little yeast of tev in the bottom of the barrel and I mixed it with the newly made water until I got unharmful juice. Then I took some threads from my fur coat and dipped them into that juice, making the grass and the flowers and the trees of the earth. And now the cake of the earth was very beautiful indeed. But I couldn't be really happy as long as I knew I was the only one to enjoy it. So I decided to offer the earth to people who could appreciate its charm. I cut a little bit from the tip of right ear and carved a man: then I cut a little bit from the tip of my left ear and carved a woman. They were wonderful and they had my own immortal blood in their veins. The tiny bits which fell down during my carving turned into animals and fish and birds... But you must know, Tarbit, that the dragons aren't the product of my hands: they are descen-

In the end I made a sort of flour of stone and I could model with it a sort of cake which you now call "earth." ...

dants of two bugs from Gudulland which fell on your earth from the fur of my coat.

Now the cake of the earth was ready, but the man and the woman couldn't enjoy life without the blessing of love. So I started doing the most delicate job I had undertaken until then: I modeled a magical bird from the transparent fume of my breath, to bind the man and woman's hearts with invisible chains. That's how Vihta was born. And since I wanted to make the air over the earth more pleasant, I made up the sky from the fume of my breath also and stuck a little golden button on it which was called Vihta's Star, so that everybody should know that the bird that was living there was the only master I've chosen for my little world. Oh, what a pity you haven't seen the earth as it was then, Tarbit! Fresh and young, it was blooming in the golden-red light and the first couple of people was discovering one wonder after another, since the world was nothing but a huge magnificent palace in which they were discovering one room after another...

And the men and the animals multiplied until I lost their number and I was happy to watch over them and grew fond even of the tiniest baby or sparrow.

But my eyes which were created to look over enormous spaces, got tired because of the straining I had imposed on them. Little by little my sight grew weak and less and less I could distinguish from the small world I've created. I felt lonely again and sad, but at least I got relief in the thought that my small world

I modeled a magical bird from the transparent fume of my breath, to bind the man and woman's hearts with invisible chains. That's how Vihta was born....

was made with love and I entrusted it to Vihta to look after.

I don't know how much time elapsed over my golden-red world... One day the whole world jerked into my hands and my eyes couldn't distinguish anything else but a greenish-grey whirl of wind rising over its golden-red light and covering it. The rumble of a strong voice reached my ears and it said: "Old giant Panca, it's a pity you've abandoned the world that you are keeping in your hands! The cities of the world are collapsing, the people are lying and cheating each other, giant Panca!" Never have I felt a stronger pain than at that moment, because my world is everything I have in my stone prison, and I've put so much love and skill into creating it, and all the best in my heart and in my mind lies in it, Tarbit. So much I cried for my little world... I asked: "Who are you, who have thrust the spear of pain in old Panca's heart?"

"I'm Ormag and my name is fear!" replied the voice in the greenish-grey whirl. Those words seemed quite queer to me. I've put wisdom and boldness into the hearts of my people. I've put high aspirations and sense of justice, but fear I haven't put as it was unknown to me and couldn't understand its power. So Ormag began to speak and speak and persuaded me that fear is what mankind needed and it was the only thing which could have saved them. But Ormag refused to take the reign over my world unless I helped him. I was ready to do anything to save my dear world, and he made me separate the earth from the sky and create the balance of the world with the earth on one pan and the sky on the other. And the agreement between us was that I would keep the balance uneven, so that the sky would look heavier and the narts' luck be favoured over mankind's, unless a man would throw his own heart on the pan of the earth to prove to me his sincerity. So much I cried for my little world then... and no tear of today can efface for me one single tear of that day, Tarbit..."

* * *

This is how Panca the giant ended his story and sighed, while Tarbit felt his heart full of an old hatred and pain. "Cheating and wicked Ormag" he said, "you'll fall down."

He took Vam's stone in his palm and looked towards the pan of the earth, far away, where his beloved Milga was waiting for him in the city of Naat with golden palaces and ruby gates. He said: "You know how much I love you, Milga. For the smile of your lips I would struggle to raise mankind to the stars... but we are living under Ormag's iron heel. Smile Milga even when I'll be gone. But don't let the narts laugh!" Then he kissed Vam's stone and the stone flew away towards the earth. Tarbit threw his own heart on the pan of the earth and his eyes had still time to see the balance of the world jerking and the earth achieving supremacy over the sky. Then his sight blurred and he fell lifeless from Panca's shoulder.

He took Vam's stone in his palm and looked towards the pan of the earth, far away, where his beloved Milga was waiting for him in the city of Naat with golden palaces and ruby gates....

But the end of this story is the beginning of another one, because Tarbit had a wife and she was still alive.

Part IV: Vam's Smile

As you know, Pil had abandoned Tarbit in the stone realm of Panca's barrel when he understood he couldn't make him his ally, and he was absolutely sure no mortal would ever be able to talk to Panca. What had happened in Nartazuba since then?

The narts had no more reason to hide the city of Naat. The cloud over the city disappeared and Ormag saw with amazement an unusual glittering in Saian's light. He sent Birgun to investigate what was going on there and the dumbfounded messenger reported that he saw a city with golden palaces and ruby gates. "Naat?" shouted Ormag and jumped from his fog-throne. His voice rumbled like thunder when he said: "You cheating, stupid narts, you've conspired against me again! You've forgotten that I'm Ormag and my name is fear! My name is written on the bottom of your damned hearts, so deep that nobody will ever be able to efface it!"

The horrified narts fell on their knees and begged for mercy, while Ormag instructed each of them how to attack the city of Naat. Then Gurz was asked to send three huge arrows towards the earth and each of them was meant to kill nine hundred and ninety-nine mortals.

But that was exactly the time when Milga told the people of the city how the narts made Tarbit disappear from the palace and the angry young people shouted: "The powerful Ormag is the enemy of Vam's people!" Gurz's arrows were stopped in the air by the tremendous power of the mortals' words. And from his chains at Nartazuba's gate, Vam said: "It's too late. Ormag! I've sworn that Nartazuba's walls will collapse and you'll regret it. And that will be!"

"Worm!" shouted Ormag and hit his forehead with the bone-axe. But Vam was immortal. And for the first time after so many years. Vam smiled... There was such a power in that quiet smile that the narts howled like frightened dogs.

Ormag made a sign towards Dumvur. The nart of the sea caused enormous billows to rise over the earth and Hudu the wind blew over the water, while Zubala covered the sky with her dark mantle. The water covered the island of the Red City, covered the ruins of Zinu, and then came over Agra. The king of Agra took up torches and brought his bags of gold on the roof of his palace. The palace was the tallest building of Agra and he waited there watching all his country drowning. Desperate mothers tried to put their babies on the roof of the king's palace, but he threw the babies down. He cut away the hands of the people who tried to cling to the roof. He made a pyramid with his bags of gold and mounted on the top of it and promised the narts to

The king of Agra took up torches and brought his bags of gold on the roof of his palace. The palace was the tallest building of Agra and he waited there watching all his country drowning....

build them temples with all his gold. But the narts had no time to listen to any mortal's words, now that Nartazuba was trembling and melting away. "Take him away!" shouted Dumvur to the waves, and the waves obeyed and took away the last mortal of Agra, the king who had once swept the floor of the palace of Zinu with the beard of his enemy and washed it with his lips.

There was no living creature left on the earth, except in the city of Naat which was glittering in the light of the maun-apples. The crazy daughters of night took Tarbit's shape and they looked with Tarbit's eyes and spoke with Tarbit's voice: "I was wrong, Milga! We have to surrender to the powerful narts!" But the bold Milga answered: "The powerful Ormag is the enemy of Vam's people! You aren't Tarbit!" Zubala's crazy daughters vanished in the night and Dumvur and Hudu attacked Naat from all sides.

"Just a moment" said the sly Pil, "Ormag would like to spare you, people of Naat, because you are the boldest and most just from the whole earth. Sacrifice to Ormag one single buffalo and Ormag will forgive you and the waters will retire."

That moment Zubala's mantle was pierced by a big light and Vam's stone came towards the city and stopped in Milga's hand. And Milga began to cry when her ears heard Tarbit's words of farewell, which came from beyond the world: "You know how much I love you, Milga. For the smile of your lips I would struggle to raise mankind to the stars... but we are living under

Ormag's iron heel. Smile Milga, even when I'll be gone. But don't let the narts laugh!"

"It's OK, Tarbit!" said Milga. Then she shouted with tears in her eyes: "The powerful Ormag is the enemy of Vam's people!" No oblation will be burnt in Naat, but our hate and pain will strike the walls of Nartazuba."

Dumvur and Hudu began to roar, but the waves round Naat rose into a round wall of water and couldn't cover the city. Then the people of Naat took each other's hands and made a circle and began to sing. Nobody had taught them that song but their hearts knew it alone. It was a wordless song, the victorious song about man's triumph over the immortal narts. It was Lua's song which she had once sang in the village of Cargand, it wasn't an urge to rebellion, but rebellion itself.

And then the whole city of Naat began to rise above the water like an enormous glittering ship... because at that moment Tarbit's heart shifted the balance of the world.

"Nartazuba's dying! It's dying!" yelled the narts.

Natazuba was collapsing, the narts looked like Mastazuba's shadows and with a last effort Ormag shouted: "I'm Ormag and my name is fear!" and threw the bone-axe of power in Milga's breast. The axe met Vam's stone and was broken like a toy. "You have no name in the city with golden palaces and ruby gates, you Greenish-Grey One!" shouted Milga.

At those words the cheating Zubala abandoned her master and hid in her palace. Saian shone again in the sky and the people of Naat saw Ormag's body dissolving and vanishing as a mist, Nartazuba disappearing far away, and the narts falling down in the sea where Mastara had to seal their eyes (because the narts were immortal only as long as their palace was immortal). The only narts who remained were Mastara, Cadumal, and Saian who lived in Mastazuba, Zubala and her crazy daughters who lived in their own dark palace, and Dumvur who couldn't be reached in his palace at the bottom of the sea.

Vam and Una's chains fell from them like dead snakes, and in the square of Naat the two people came hand in hand. Mastara said: "You have broken the ice of my heart once, Vam, and I'm grateful for that. You and Una will remain in the middle of your people." And Mastara didn't touch their eyes with her back seal, but with her white fingers. Vam and Una turned into two marble statues, standing hand in hand in the middle of their people and smiling for ever.

Seven days and seven nights did the city of Naat fly over the earth, until the waters came back into their former beds.

But the end of this story is the beginning of a new one, because Vam's people are still alive and they are making up their own story just now. And who knows, maybe one day they'll acquire immortality again and they'll be able to rise into the air and reach Vihta's Star...

HISTRIA

BOOKS